The Hopes and Dreams Series
Chinese-Americans

For Gold and Blood

A story based on history

Second Edition

Tana Reiff

Illustrations by Tyler Stiene

PRO LINGUA ASSOCIATES

Pro Lingua Associates, Publishers

74 Cotton Mill Hill, Suite A315
Brattleboro, Vermont 05301 USA
Office: 802 257 7779
Orders: 800 366 4775
E-mail: orders@ProLinguaAssociates.com
SAN: 216-0579
Webstore: www.ProLinguaAssociates.com

Text ISBN 13: 978-0-86647-380-4; 10: 0-86647-380-7
Audio CD ISBN 13: 978-0-86647-381-1; 10: 0-86647-381-5

The first edition of this book was originally published by Fearon Education, a division of David S. Lake Publishers, Belmont, California, Copyright © 1989, later by Pearson Education. This, the second edition, has been revised and redesigned.

The cover and illustrations are by Tyler Stiene. The book was set and designed by Tana Reiff, consulting with A.A. Burrows, using the Adobe *Century Schoolbook* typeface for the text. This is a digital adaptation of one of the most popular faces of the twentieth century. Century's distinctive roman and italic fonts and its clear, dark strokes and serifs were designed, as the name suggests, to make schoolbooks easy to read. The display font used on the cover and titles is a 21st-century digital invention titled Telugu. It is designed to work on all digital platforms and with Indic scripts. Telugu is named for the Telugu people in southern India and their widely spoken language. This is a simple, strong, and interesting sans serif display font.

This book was printed and bound by KC Book Manufacturing in North Kansas City, Missouri. Printed in the United States. Second Edition, Fourth Printing

---

The Hopes and Dreams Series
by Tana Reiff

The Magic Paper (Mexican-Americans)
For Gold and Blood (Chinese-Americans)
Nobody Knows (African-Americans)
Little Italy (Italian-Americans)
Hungry No More (Irish-Americans)
Sent Away (Japanese-Americans)
Two Hearts (Greek-Americans)
Old Ways, New Ways (Jewish-Americans)

Contents

1 Leaving Home

Guangdong Province, China, 1851

"They call it
Gold Mountain!"
Soo Lee said
to his brother Ping.
"It's a place
across the ocean.
I think its name
is California.
People with nothing
get rich fast!
They find gold
in the hills
and in the streams!"

"Look at us!"
Soo continued.
"Since the war,
we have had
no real home.
Our family is poor.
All of us
cannot keep living
in this houseboat.

Let's go
to Gold Mountain!"

    "How can you
talk like this?"
Ping asked his brother.
"China is the center
of the Earth.
Our family is here.
Anyway, we could not leave
even if we wanted to.
The country
will not let us go."

    "There are ways
to get out,"
said Soo.
"We can pay
the men at the port.
They will get us
onto a ship
and out of the country."

    Ping Lee
was not sure
he liked Soo's plan.
But he liked the idea
of finding gold.

Going to California
could help
the whole family.
He and Soo
could send money home.
In a few years
they could come
back to China.

Soo kept talking.
He had not felt this happy
since before the war.

At last Ping said,
"You are right.
We should go.
We are young and strong.
We are the only ones
who can help our family."

The Lee family
was very large.
The brothers told them
about their plan.
Everyone wanted
to raise money
for the trip.
It would help everyone.

Ma Ma Lee
wanted to give her boys
her jade stone.
It was
the one special thing
she owned.
It would
keep them safe,
far from home.
But she sold it
and gave her boys
the money
instead of the stone.

Uncle Wang
sold his only cow.
Someday, he would try
to buy another one.

In a few months,
the family
had enough money
for Soo and Ping
to go to California.

The brothers
went to Hong Kong.

They paid a man
to get them
onto a ship.
Deep in the ship's hold,
they sat on brown mats
with hundreds
of other people.

    Two months later,
the ship reached America.
A Chinese man
met the ship
in California.
He gave each man
a pick, a shovel, and a pan.
They could pay
for these tools
when they found gold.
The Chinese man
showed the young men
how to use the tools.
Then he showed them
how to go
to the gold fields.

2 Finding Gold

Soo and Ping
went to work
for a gold-mining company.
The American men
showed them
how to find gold.
Soo and Ping
learned fast.
They picked for gold
up and down the hills.
They used flat pans
to find gold
in streams.

Sure enough,
they found gold.
Some were nuggets
as big as a finger.
Most of the gold
was like dust.
The company
let the workers
keep half of any gold
that they found.

The Chinese workers
did not look or act
like the Americans.
The Chinese men
wore blue coats
and big, wide hats.
Their shoes
had heavy wood bottoms.
Each man wore
a long tail
of black hair
down his back.
Each carried
a long pole
with a bag
tied to the end.
Inside the bag
were clothes, food,
and a mat.

They ate
with two sticks
instead of a fork.
Every night,
they slept
on their mats,
away from the main camp.

The Americans laughed
at the Chinese men.
"You look like clowns
with yellow skin!"
they called out.

Soo and Ping
did not understand
every word of this talk.
But they knew
that the men
were making fun of them.

"Don't listen to them,"
Soo said to Ping.
"We are finding
little bits of gold.
We will be rich,
all of us!"

"This is too good
to be true!"
said Ping.
"I cannot believe
we are finding real gold!"

"I told you so,
little brother!"
said Soo.
"Soon the whole family
can come to California.
After we pay
for our tools."

"No, no!"
said Ping.
"I am homesick.
I want to send money
to our family
and then go back
to China.
That was our plan!"

"We will see
what happens,"
said Soo.
"Maybe we will
be lucky and
strike it rich.
But for now,
we must live
in this country.
And we must learn English."

"You are right,"
said Ping.
"Each day
we must learn
some new English words."

A few weeks later,
Ping made a big strike.
It was late
in the day.
"Look here!"
he called to Soo.
"Have you ever seen
such a large piece of gold?"

Soo held
the shiny nugget.
It was as big
as his hand.
It was almost pure gold.

The news spread
like wildfire.
Everyone in the camp
wanted to take a look
at the very large nugget.

"That's a big strike,"
said the camp boss.

"You get half,
we get half,"
Soo said in English.

"Not on a nugget that big!"
laughed the boss.
"Now, you and your brother
get out of here!
Leave this camp!
Now!"

Ping turned to Soo.
"There is no use
in fighting,"
he said in Chinese.

"We must leave."

Soo was angry.
They had a deal—
50-50.

The boss was not
being fair.
Ping should get
half of the gold
that he had found.

  The sun
was setting
over the mountain.
Soo and Ping
tied their bags
to their poles.
By the light
of the moon
they left the camp,
like a flash
in the pan.

3 Moving On

Soo and Ping walked
for three hours.
Then they
lay on their mats
for the night.
They had no idea
where they were.

The next day,
they walked again.
Before long,
they came upon
another gold camp.
The boss
let them
join the gang.

Most of the Americans
liked working
in the hills.
Soo and Ping
liked working
in the water.
Their feet
felt as cold as ice.

Over their heads,
the sun
felt as hot as fire.
Soo and Ping
did not mind.
Their wide hats helped
to keep them cool.
They thought about
their family back home.

The work
was very slow.
They panned
all day long,
looking for gold.
They found gold dust,
here and there.

"We will never
strike it big here,"
said Soo.

"That's all right,"
said Ping.
"Here we are safe.
With no big strike
like before,
the camp boss
will not drive us out."

But as weeks went by,
they found
less and less gold.
One morning
the camp boss
talked to the gang.

"The gold
is running out,"
he told them.
"There is not enough work
for everyone now.
So you Chinamen
must leave the camp."

Once again
Soo was angry.
"The first boss
drove us out
for finding too much gold,"
he said to Ping.
"The second boss
drives us out
for not finding enough!"

There was nothing
they could do.
The camp boss
would not let them stay.
So Soo and Ping
packed their bags.

"Let's head north,"
said Soo.
"We will find gold.
We will pick over places
others before us left.
We don't need
to work in a gang.
We'll find gold
on our own!"

That is
what they did.
They did not
strike it rich.
All they found
was gold dust.

They did that
for twelve long years.
The gold dust
kept them working.
But there was not
enough money
to send home.
And not nearly enough
to bring anyone
to America.

Then even the gold dust
became hard to find.

One day Ping said,
"I want to go home.
Let's go back to China."

"We can't go home,"
said Soo.
"Not now.
Not yet."

"Listen,"
Soo went on.
"I heard
they are starting
to build a railroad.
They need workers.
I'm tired of
trying to find gold.
The gold is gone.
I'd like to go
and build the railroad."

4 The Railroad

"Come with me,"
Soo said to Ping.
"Let's build the railroad."

"I still want
to look for gold,"
Ping answered.
"We may get lucky
one of these days."

"I'm finished with gold,"
said Soo.
"You go your way
and I'll go mine."
Soo was sorry
that his brother
would not come with him.

"Some day
we will meet again,"
said Ping.
"Good luck, my brother."

They hugged
for a long time.
Then they said goodbye.

Soo went to work
on the new railroad.
He joined a gang
of 10,000 men.
The American men
were paid $35 a month.
The Chinese men
were paid $25 a month.
And the Chinese
had to pay
for their food.
The Americans did not.

Soo and the other men
had never worked so hard.
They blasted
through rock,
inch by inch.
They made long, flat beds
of stones.
They set wooden ties
on top of the stones.

They laid heavy rails
over the ties.
They drilled holes
for the spikes
that held the rails
to the ties.
They started work
at the first light of day.
They did not stop
until it was dark.
Day by day,
they worked their way
toward the high mountains.

At Donner Pass,
the work became
even harder.
The mountain pass
was covered with snow.
New snow fell
every day.

In the high mountains,
the workers
lived and worked
under 40 feet of snow.

To get air,
they cut holes
through the snow.
Every morning
they cut a road
in the snow.
This was the only way
to get to the workplace.
Many men died
in that cold, hard winter.

The work
became still worse
later that year.
At the top
of a mountain
Soo was put
into a big basket.
The basket
came down the mountain
on a rope.
From inside the basket
Soo drilled holes,
by hand,
into the rock
of the mountain.

He placed gunpowder
into the holes.
He lit the powder
with a match.
Then he pulled himself up
as fast as he could.
He got out of the way
before the rock blew up.

One night
the Chinese workers
were talking.
The American workers
could not understand them.

"This is not fair,"
said one man.
"We work very hard.
We Chinese
do the most dangerous work.
We work more hours.
Why don't *we*
get $35 a month?
Why don't *we*
get free food?"

"Because we are Chinese,"
said another man.

"Let's change this!"
said Soo Lee.
"Let's go on strike!
We will stop working.
We will ask
for $40 a month
and free food.
We will ask
for shorter work days.
They must give us
what we want!"

The next morning,
the Chinese workers
stayed in the camp.
They did not
come out to work.
"Eight hours a day
is good for white men.
It is also good
for Chinese men,"
Soo told the boss.

But the boss
did not care
about the strike.
He used his power
against the Chinese workers.
He did not let them
buy any food.
They had nothing to eat.

The strike was over,
one day after it started.

5 San Francisco

Ping had gone north
to Oregon.
New gold fields
were up there.
For over a year,
he panned the streams.
He picked over places
that had been panned
and left behind.

Ping worked hard.
But his luck
did not get better.
He did not find
enough gold to live on.
And at night,
when he looked up
at the stars,
he felt so alone.

He began to think
that Soo had been right.

Maybe he should have
gone with him
to build the railroad.

Ping knew one thing.
He had to find
a better way
to make money.
Then one day
he had an idea.

Ping had worked
in many parts
of California and Oregon.
In all of those places
he saw few women.
He knew
that most men
had come here
to make money.
Women did not come along.
Back in China,
women had washed
the men's clothes.
Here in the west
there was no one
to do this work.

Men who had money
sent their dirty clothes
to China or Hawaii.
Women in those far places
washed the clothes
and mailed them back.
It cost eight dollars
to wash twelve shirts.
That was a lot of money
in those days.

Like the other men,
Ping Lee thought
that washing clothes
was women's work.
But maybe
he could make some money
doing laundry.

So Ping decided
to start a laundry.
He went to San Francisco
and opened a shop.

He found a place
on Grant Avenue.
It was two rooms.

He set up the laundry
in the front room.
He lived
in the back room.
Ping's new laundry
was not big.
It was not pretty.
But he was
the only one
who saw it.
He picked up
the dirty clothes
at people's homes.
Then he dropped off
the clean clothes.

He needed
only a few things
to get started.
He bought soap.
A brush.
A washing sink.
An iron.
A coal stove
to heat the iron
and make hot water.
He made
an ironing board.

Ping had learned
how to pan for gold.
Now he learned
how to run a laundry.

He started working
at 4:00 in the morning.
First, he washed clothes
in very hot water
in the sink.
Then he hung
the wet clothes
on strong wires
to dry by the stove.
Next, he put them
into big baskets
all over the room.

He kept
a bowl of water
next to the ironing board.
He put his head
into the bowl.
He filled his mouth
with water.
As he shook his head,
he blew the water
over a shirt.

The shirt had to be
just wet enough,
not too wet.

The iron sat
on the hot stove.
It was eight pounds.
Ping lifted
the heavy iron.
He spat on it
to make sure
it was hot enough.
Then, very fast,
he ironed shirts.
He had burns
all over his hands.

He added up
each person's bill
on rows of beads
on the wall.
He worked
until 10:00 every night.

From the start
of his business,
Ping made money.

He had seen a need
and he filled it.
But every day,
his brother Soo
was on Ping's mind.
Where could Soo be?
Was he all right?
Was he alive?
Would the brothers
ever see each other again?

6 Two Lives

Ping joined
a group of families
from different parts of
China. It was called
the Six Companies.
It was named
for six places in China.
The members
helped each other.
When new Chinese people
came to California,
the group welcomed them.
They helped them
to find work
and a place to live.
They also tried
to fight American laws
against Chinese people.

These days,
Ping could not think
about going back home.

He gave up that idea
a long time ago.
He could not become
an American citizen.
He could not vote.
He could not marry.
All because he was Chinese.
He just kept working hard
at his business.

All of Ping's hard work
paid off.
He made some money.
Now, at last,
he could bring
some people from his family
to California.
His uncle's son Chen
was the first to come.

"Welcome to California!"
Ping told the young man.
"The last time
I saw you,
you were a little boy."

Ping made
a place for Chen
to live with him
in the back room.
The Chinese Six Companies
found Chen a job
in a cigar factory.
He worked at night
in the laundry.

More family members
came after that.
Ping made room
for all of them.
He nailed boards
to the walls
of the back room.
Everyone had a board
to sleep on.

Other Chinese people
in San Francisco
also brought family.
Grant Avenue
became the heart
of Chinatown.

Little by little,
Chinatown grew
into a little city
inside a big city.
Shops sold
ducks, rice, beans, tea,
flowers, and herbs.
It was a busy place.
Ping didn't even know
most of these people.

Still, no word from Soo.
"A lot of Chinese died
building the railroad,"
Ping told the family.
"Maybe Soo is dead."

But far from California,
in the state of Utah,
Soo Lee was alive.
It was 1869.
The long railroad
was almost finished.
Workers from the east
met workers from the west.
The two long tracks
they had built
came together as one.

"Be gone now, Chinamen!"
shouted the boss.
"Your work is done!"

Suddenly,
Soo Lee was out of work.
He had no place to go.

There was a big party
where the railroad
came together.
The president of the railroad
drove the last spike
into the track.
That last spike was pure gold.
The railroad now reached
from ocean to ocean.

Chinese workers
had built most of the track
coming from the west.
But the Chinese
were sent away
before the party.
The finished railroad
was shown to the world
without the people
who had built it.

7   Trouble in the City

Soo Lee
headed for San Francisco
to find work.
White workers
from the shoe factories
were on strike.
Chinese workers
were filling the jobs.

Soo wondered
about his brother.
He did not know
that Ping Lee
was in San Francisco.

So many Chinese workers
had come to San Francisco.
Some white people
grew to hate them.
They believed
that Chinese people
were taking their jobs.

Soo got a job
in a shoe factory.
He didn't like it.
The pay was low.
He wanted
to work outside.
He was not happy.

At night,
Soo played cards
with other men.
It was a game
called fan-tan.
Some nights
he won money.
Most nights
he lost money.
He had nothing else
to do after work.
The hall
was like a club.
It was called a tong.

Young Chinese girls
started working
at the hall.

Going to the hall
and being part
of the tong
was so much better
than being alone.

Then one night
one of the men
talked to Soo.
"This tong
will soon control
all the card games
in Chinatown,"
the man said.
"We have work for you
if you want it.
It can be dangerous.
What do you say?"

"Why not?"
Soo said.
"I've never been afraid
to play my luck."

Soo visited halls
all over town
for the tong.
He checked on
the games.
He took
a cut of the money
from the card tables.
He gave
part of the money
to the tong.
He kept part of it
for himself.

Then one day,
all the Chinese people
were told to leave
the shoe factory.
The strike was over.
Soo began to work full time
with the tong.

"Trouble is growing
in Chinatown,"
the tong president told Soo.
"White people
are coming here.
They are hurting
Chinese people.
They beat us up.
They rob us
on the street
and in our shops.
This must stop!
I want you
to find ways
to help our people.
We will protect them.
And they will pay us
for protection."

Four blocks away,
Ping ran his laundry.
Late one night,
he began closing up,
just like always.

He cleaned up
and put things
in their places.
He counted money.
He walked toward the door
to lock up.
Everyone who lived
in the back room
was out working.
Ping was alone.

Suddenly, three men
pushed on the door.
Ping tried
to push back.
He was not strong enough
to push away
three big men.

8 The Laundry

The three men
pushed their way
into the laundry.
They pushed Ping
back toward the stove.
Ping felt a gun
pressing on his back.

"Hand over
your money!"
they shouted.
"You have no right
to make money
in our country."

"I do not take jobs
away from you,"
said Ping.
"I only wash clothes.
No one but Chinese
wants to wash clothes."

The three men
did not listen
to what Ping said.
"Give us your money
or we will kill you,"
said one of the men,
pointing his gun.

"Take my money,"
Ping said.
"But please
do not hurt me!
I have a big family
to take care of."

The second man
took the money.
The third man
hit Ping over the head.
He fell down
to the floor.

With guns and sticks
the three men
smashed everything in sight.

They laughed
the whole time.
Then they ran out.

The news
reached the tong
the next day.
A laundry
on Grant Avenue
had been smashed.
The owner
had been robbed.
He was badly hurt
but not dead.

"I want to go
to the laundry,"
Soo told the tong.
"I want to tell
the owner
how we can help him.
He can pay us
each month.
We will make sure
he is never hurt again."

When Ping woke up
it was time
to start work.
His head hurt,
but the men
had not shot him.
He looked
at what they had done.
The place
was a mess.

Just then,
Ping looked out
to the street.
He saw a man walking
toward the laundry.
He knew the face.
It was no longer
a young face.
But he knew for sure
that it was his brother.
The man at the door
was Soo Lee.

9 Family

Ping opened
his arms.
"My brother!"
he cried.
"My long-lost brother!"

"It is so good
to see you!"
said Soo.
"How many years
has it been?
I should have guessed
you were in Chinatown!"

"Yes, I am here,"
said Ping.
"And I have brought over
more of our family!
But why are *you* here?
Was it by chance
that you were walking
down Grant Avenue?"

"No," said Soo.
"I have been
in San Francisco
for a little while.
I came
to your laundry
because my tong
wants to help you.
We know
the white men
hit your place
last night.
The tong
wants you to pay us
to keep trouble away.
But you are my brother.
I cannot take your money.
I will make sure
that you are not hurt."

"I have heard of things
that the tongs do!"
said Ping.
"I will give no pay-offs!
No dirty money!

But Soo, my brother,
I am not surprised
that you are in a tong.
You always were the one
to play your luck!
Not me.
I am happy
to be part
of the Six Companies,
not a tong."

"Your group of families
holds too much power,"
said Soo.
"But it is too slow to act.
In Chinatown,
the tongs
get things done—now!
You wait, my brother.
The tongs
will rule Chinatown
in the end."

Just then,
Chen walked in.

"Ah, Chen!"
said Ping.
"Meet your cousin.
This is my brother, Soo."

Soo and Chen
shook hands.

"I am glad
to meet one of my blood,"
said Soo.
"Let me know
if you ever need help."

"Thank you,"
said Chen.

"Where have you
been all night?"
Ping asked Chen.

"At the fan-tan hall,"
said the young man.

"Why do you go there?"
Ping wanted to know.

"To play fan-tan,
of course,"
Chen said.
"I love that card game.
And the girls.
The sing-song girls."

"I don't want you
to play cards
and spend money
on sing-song girls!
I don't want you
in that tong!"
Ping said loudly.

Soo laughed.
"Those girls are
the only Chinese women
in San Francisco!
Let the boy go
and have a good time."

Ping did not like
what he was hearing.
But Soo was older,
so he said nothing.

"Maybe sometime
I will see you
at the hall,"
Soo said to Chen.
"Now, Ping,
let's talk
about your business.
I want you
to be safe."

"No strings?"
Ping asked.

"No money,
if that's what you mean,"
said Soo.
"We are family.
Blood comes first."

10 The Flower Girl

That night,
Soo went
to the fan-tan hall.

"Hey, Soo!"
a tong friend
called to him
across the room.
"Look over there!
Another man
is sitting with your girl!"

Soo saw the girl
he liked the most
on the other side
of the large room.
She was beautiful.
Soo loved
her long, black hair.
She always wore
a flower in it.
Everyone called her
the Flower Girl.

The Flower Girl
was very young.
Soo was almost 40.
He watched the girl
as she talked
with the young man.

Soo started
to walk toward her.
Then he suddenly stopped.
The Flower Girl
was talking with Chen!

"Do you want some help?"
the tong friend asked Soo.
"Do you want us
to send that boy home?"

Soo was ready
to say no.
But it was too late.
His tong friends headed
toward the Flower Girl's table.
They pulled Chen
off his chair.
They pushed him
toward the front door.

"Keep your hands
off the Flower Girl!"
the tong men told Chen.

Just then,
another man stood up.
"What do you think
you are doing?"
shouted the man.
"That young man
is a Lee.
Get your hands
off him!"

Suddenly,
there was a fight.
Tables and chairs
flew all over the room.

The fight
went out into the street.
It was starting to look
like a small war.

Young Chen Lee
headed away
from the hall.
He had a small cut
on his face.
A little blood
was on his shirt.
Worse than that,
he had to go home
and face Uncle Ping.

11 Big Changes

"I don't like this,"
Ping said to Soo.
"Blood should not
fight blood.
I am first and always
a Lee.
So are you.
You said it yourself,
Blood comes first."

"The fight
over the Flower Girl
was not my idea,"
said Soo.
"But I do believe
in the tong.
If the tong
can help you or me,
that's good.
If it cannot,
then I am sorry.
You will have
no protection."

"There is a way
you can stop fights
over girls,"
said Ping.
"Find Chen a wife.
Bring over a good woman
from China."

"I will do
the best I can,"
said Soo.
"It won't be easy.
The Americans
are trying to stop
Chinese people
from coming here.
We must work fast."

Soo and the tong
knew how to work fast.
But this time
they could not work
fast enough.
A law passed
that no new Chinese workers
could come to America.

Under the new law,
women and children
could not come
if their men worked
in factories or farms.
Only business owners
could bring their families
over from China.

"There is only one way
to bring a woman
for Chen,"
Soo told Ping.
"He must stop working
in the factory.
He must run
his own business.
Then we must say
he was married
in China."

Ping did not like
to make up a lie.
He had
his own idea.

"Chen,"
he began.
"I am getting old.
I will give you
my laundry.
You may run it
as your own.
I will work for you
as long as I can."

So young Chen
took over the laundry business.
Soo made papers
saying Chen was married
back in China.

In a few months
Chen had a wife.
Her name was Chan.
At last,
the Lees
had a woman
in the house.
And, for now,
there was peace
in the family.

12 War and Peace

Another new law
said that all Chinese
must sign up
and carry cards.
The leader
of the Six Companies
told Chinese people
not to sign up.
The tongs
did not want
the Six Companies
to have that power.
They put money
on the leader's head.
Again there was fighting.

From the time
they were children,
it was never easy
for Ping to stand up
to his brother.
But now he had
something important to say.

"Blood must not fight blood,"
Ping told Soo.
"I have said this before.
We cannot let this be.
You and I are brothers.
We can be the bridge
between the groups.
Let us work together
for peace in Chinatown."

"Yes," said Soo.
"Let us work together.
We are too old
to fight in the street.
But we are not too old
to talk."

The Six Companies
lost the battle
over the new law.
But the tong wars
went on for years.
Tongs fought tongs
over who would run
the fan-tan halls
and other businesses.
Oceans of blood
ran in the streets.

Soo and Ping Lee
had done all they could
to keep blood
from fighting blood.

By 1906,
Soo and Ping
were old men.
One morning,
very early,
both were sleeping.
Soo felt water
falling on his head.
He woke up
right away.
Everything in the room
began to shake.

Soo knew right away
it was an earthquake.
A water pipe
over his room
had cracked wide open.
Water fell down
all over him.

He got out of bed.
It took a few minutes.
He could not move
as fast as he did
when he was young.

He pulled on
his clothes.
Then he headed
to the laundry.

Ping and the family
were standing outside.
The laundry
was on fire.
Soon much of the city
was on fire.
Many of the buildings
burned down.
Chinatown was gone.

San Francisco
was not the same
after the earthquake
of 1906.

But in some ways
it was good
for the Chinese.
With Chinatown gone,
there was nothing left
to fight over.
The tong wars ended,
and a new Chinatown
was built.

   The earthquake
helped the Chinese
in another way.
Important papers
were lost in the fires.
No one could know for sure
which Chinese were born
in America.

   "Now I can bring over
my son from China!"
said Soo.

   "What do you mean?"
asked Ping.
"You do not have a son!"

"I can have
a 'paper son'!"
said Soo.
"Without real papers,
I can say
I had a son in China.
No one will ever know
if it's true or not!"

"You always have
a bright idea!"
Ping laughed.
"You will never stop,
will you?"

Before Soo died,
he brought over
three young men.
This made him
a happy old man.

Ping was glad
to have Chen's family.
Chen and Chan
had five children.
Ping was like
a grandfather to them.

Peace and real hope came
for the Chinese in America.
But only after Soo and Ping
were gone.

The day came in 1944
when the Chinese
could become American citizens.
Chen and Chan's children
were among the first.

Chen and Chan
told their children
the story of the brothers,
Soo and Ping.
They never forgot
that they had paid
a high price for peace.

It was paid on Gold Mountain.
It was paid on the railroad tracks.
It was paid at the laundry.
It was paid during the tong wars.
It was paid in the earthquake.
It was paid in blood.
It was paid by many hard years of work,
until it brought the Chinese in America
a better life.

Glossary

Definitions and examples of certain words and
terms used in the story

Chapter 1 — Leaving Home page 1

at last — Finally; after time has passed.
  At last, Ping said ...

raise (to raise) — To collect money for a
  specific purpose or cause.
  Everyone wanted to raise money.

instead of — In the place of or as a substitute for.
  *(She) gave her boys the money instead of the
  stone.*

hold — The inside lower part of a ship,
  usually the place for goods.
  ... deep in the ship's hold.

pick — A sharp-pointed tool for breaking things.
  He gave each man a pick ...

shovel — A tool like a spoon for digging and
  moving dirt, stones, and other material.
  He gave each man a pick, a shovel, and a pan.

pan — A large round plate. Dirt and stones
  are placed in the pan and shaken to see if there
  are pieces of gold among the dirt and stones.
  He gave each man a pick, a shovel, and a pan.

Chapter 2 — Finding Gold page 6

nuggets — Pieces of gold.
Some were nuggets as big as a finger.

dust — Very small pieces.
Most of the gold was like dust.

pole — A long, thin piece of wood or metal.
Each carried a long pole.

camp — The place where the workers lived
in very simple buildings.
They slept … away from the main camp.

clowns — Circus people in silly colorful
clothes; they do silly things. *You look like
clowns.*

making fun of (to make fun of) — To
laugh at, tease, or make jokes about someone.
The men were making fun of them.

homesick — Wanting to be at home when
one is far away from home.
I am homesick.

(to) strike it rich — To suddenly find something very valuable and become rich.
Maybe we will be lucky and strike it rich.

shiny — Bright, reflective, colorful.
Soo held the shiny nugget.

pure — Completely; nothing else in it.
It was almost pure gold.

spread (to spread) — To move and cover quickly from place to place.
The news spread like wildfire.

wildfire — A forest or brush fire that moves very fast.
The news spread like wildfire.

no use — No good result or hope for a good solution.
There is no use in fighting.

flash in the pan — An event or situation that happens or occurs very quickly.
... they left the camp like a flash in the pan.

Chapter 3 — Moving On   page 13

gang — A group of people, usually men.
The boss let them join the gang.

panned (to pan) — To use a pan to find gold. Dirt and stones are put in the pan and shaken.
They panned all day long.

drive (us) out (to drive out) — To force people to leave a place.
... the camp boss will not drive us out.

running out (to run out) — To become less and less.
The gold is running out.

on our own — By ourselves; without help.
We'll find gold on our own!

Chapter 4 — The Railroad page 19

hugged (to hug) — To hold another person close to one's body.
They hugged for a long time.

blasted (to blast) — To use an explosive to destroy something.
They blasted through rock, inch by inch.

ties — The pieces of wood that the rails are attached to.
They set wooden ties on top of the stones.

rails — The iron bars that wheels run on.
They laid heavy rails over the ties.

drilled (to drill) — To use a tool (called a drill) that makes a hole in wood or metal.
They drilled holes for the spikes.

spikes — Sharp metal pins that hold things together; large nails.
They drilled holes for the spikes.

gunpowder — An explosive material. It can be used to blast rocks.
He placed gunpowder into the holes.

blew up (blow up) — To explode.
He got out of the way before the rock blew up.

go on strike (to go on strike) — To refuse to
work until a goal is achieved, usually better pay
and working conditions.
Let's go on strike! We will stop working.

Chapter 5 — San Francisco page 26

dropped off (to drop off) — To leave
something at a place.
Then he dropped off the clean clothes.

iron — A tool held in the hand to press on clothes
to make them smooth.
He bought … an iron.

ironing board — A flat piece of wood
covered with a heavy cloth. The clothes are
placed on the board and pressed smooth.
He made an ironing board.

spat (to spit) — To expel "water" from the mouth.
He spat on it …

burns — Places on the skin hurt by something
very hot.
He had burns all over his hands.

Chapter 6 — Two Lives page 33

paid off (to pay off) — To have a successful
result.
All of Ping's hard work paid off.

nailed (to nail) — To attach things together using a sharp metal pin (a nail).
He nailed boards to the walls.

Chapter 7 — Trouble in the City page 38

checked on (to check on) — To inspect and make sure things are going well.
He checked on the games.

a cut of — With money, it usually means a specific amount or percentage of the whole.
He took a cut of the money.

pushed (to push) on/back/away — To use the hands and body forcefully against something.
Suddenly three men pushed on the door.
Ping tried to push back. He was not strong enough to push away three big men.

Chapter 8 — The Laundry page 44

pressing (to press) — To use force (pressure) against or on something.
Ping felt a gun pressing on his back.

smashed (to smash) — To hit and destroy something.
The three men smashed everything in sight.

in sight — Everything that can be seen. (Here, everything in the laundry).
The three men smashed everything in sight.

mess — Not in good condition; broken, damaged.
The place was a mess.

Chapter 9 — Family page 48

pay-offs — Money given for a favor or special treatment, often for protection.
I will give no pay-offs!

blood — People (or a person) who are related to each other, in the same family.
I am glad to meet one of my blood.

no strings — Free of requirements or responsibilities.
"No strings?" Ping asked.

Chapter 10 — The Flower Girl page 54

flew (to fly) — To go from one place to another through the air.
Tables and chairs flew all over the room.

Chapter 11 — Big Changes   page 58

passed (to pass) — To be officially approved and made legal.
A law passed ...

run (to run) a business — To operate or manage a business.
He must run his own business.

Chapter 12 — War and Peace   page 62

put money on someone's head — To offer money to anyone who can hurt or kill a person.
They put money on the leader's head.

stand up to — To not agree with or not do something another person wants.
It was never easy for Ping to stand up to his brother.

shake — To move back and forth rapidly.
Everything in the room began to shake.

cracked (to crack) — To break.
A water pipe ... had cracked wide open.

pulled on (to pull on) — To get dressed.
He pulled on his clothes.